Spiny Animals

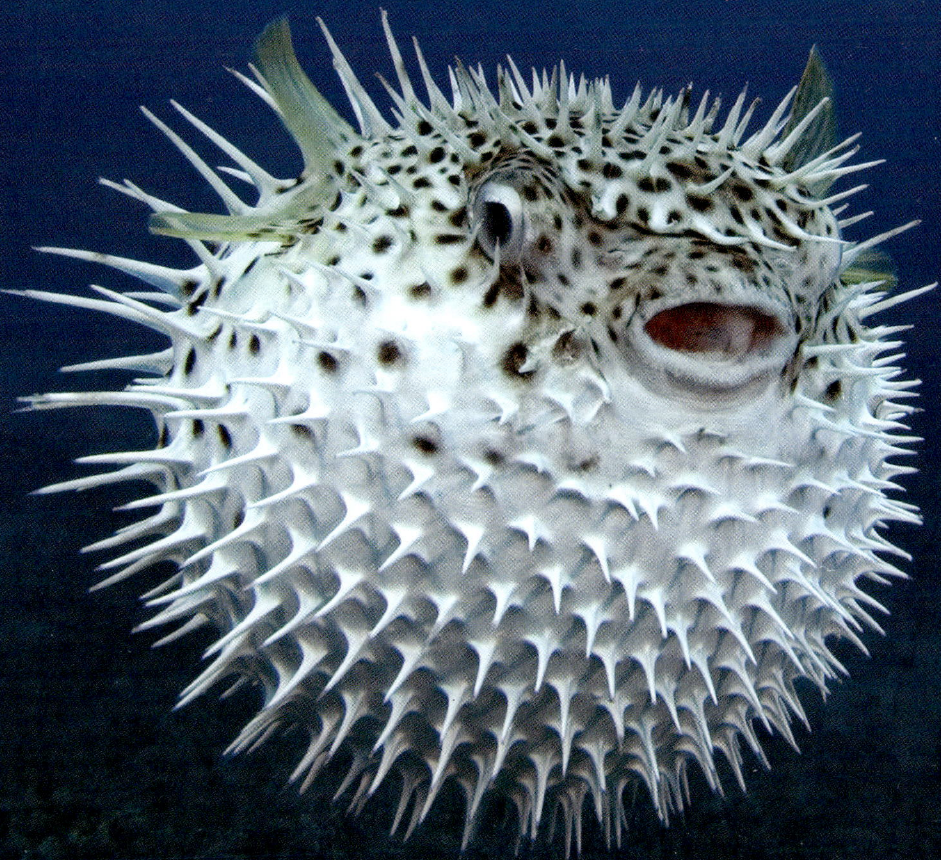

By Karen Latchana Kenney

Learn to Read
Frequent repetition of sentence structures, high frequency words, and familiar topics provide ample support for brand new readers. Approximately 100 words.

Read Independently
Repetition is mixed with varied sentence structures and 6 to 8 content words per book are introduced with photo labels and picture glossary supports. Approximately 150 words.

Read to Know More
These books feature a higher text load with additional nonfiction features such as more photos, timelines, and text divided into sections. Approximately 250 words.

Accelerated Reader methodology uses Level A instead of Pre1. We have chosen to change it for ease of understanding by potential users.

Amicus Readers hardcover editions published by **Amicus.** P.O. Box 1329, Mankato, Minnesota 56004
www.amicuspublishing.us

U.S. publication copyright © 2012 Amicus.
International copyright reserved in all countries.
No part of this book may be reproduced in any form without written permission from the publisher.

Series Editor — Rebecca Glaser
Book Editor — Wendy Dieker
Series Designer — Kia Adams
Book Designer — Heather Dreisbach
Photo Researcher — Heather Dreisbach

Printed in the United States of America at Corporate Graphics in North Mankato, Minnesota.

1022 3-2011

Library of Congress Cataloging-in-Publication Data
Kenney, Karen Latchana.
  Spiny animals / by Karen Latchana Kenney.
    p. cm. – (Amicus readers. Our animal world)
  Includes index.
  Summary: "A Level 1 Amicus Reader that describes different spiny animals and explains how their exteriors protect them from other animals. Includes comprehension activity"–Provided by publisher.
  ISBN 978-1-60753-144-9 (library binding)
  1. Animals–Juvenile literature. 2. Spines (Zoology)–Juvenile literature. I. Title.
  QL49.K426 2011
  591.47'7–dc22
                                                    2010033477

RiverStream Publishing reprinted by arrangement with Appleseed Editions Ltd.

1 2 3 4 5 CG 16 15 14 13
RiverStream Publishing—Corporate Graphics, Mankato, MN—062013—1031CGSP13

Table of Contents

Animals with Spines   4

Picture Glossary   20

What Do You Remember?   22

Ideas for Parents and Teachers   23

Index and Web Sites   24

What do spines say? They tell animals to stay away! A sea urchin's spiny shell keeps it safe from hungry fish.

When sharks are near, a puffer fish gulps water. It becomes a big spiny ball. Sharks don't want to eat it.

A porcupine has sharp quills. It sticks up its quills when it is scared. The porcupine looks bigger.

Spines cover the spiny anteater. It curls into a spiny ball. The spines keep it safe from foxes that want to eat it.

A short-horned lizard's flat body has many spikes. If the spikes don't keep danger away, it can shoot blood from its eyes!

Spiny scales run down the marine iguana's back. Animals stay away because this lizard looks scary. But it eats plants from the sea.

Some caterpillars have hollow spines. Each one has poison in it. The spines sting animals that touch them.

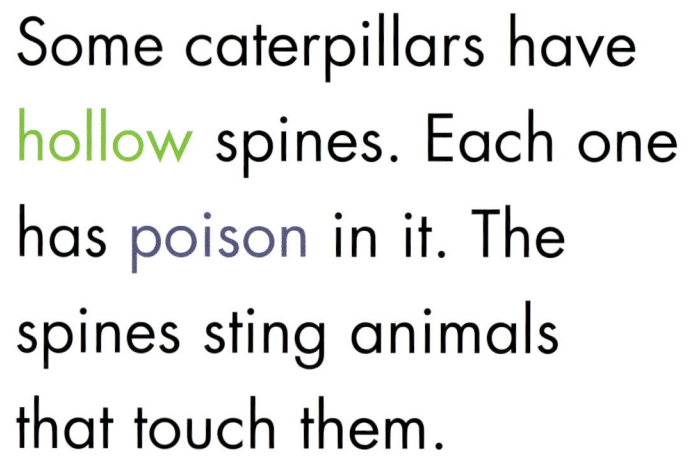

16

18

A spiny spider's body looks sharp! In nature, spines keep other animals away. If you see spines, what do you do?

Picture Glossary

hollow
having an empty space inside

poison
a liquid that can hurt or kill another animal if touched or eaten

quill
a long, pointed spine on a porcupine or hedgehog

scale
small pieces of hard skin that cover a fish, snake, or lizard

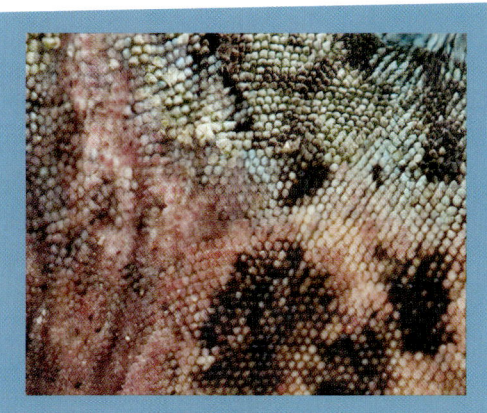

spine
a hard, sharp, pointy growth on some animals

What Do You Remember?

Look at each animal pair and answer the question.

Which animal gulps water to puff up?

Which animal has spiny scales?

Which animal has quills?

If you don't remember, read through the book again for the answers.

Ideas for Parents and Teachers

Books 6 through 10 in the RiverStream Readers Level 2 Series introduce concepts in the animal world and explore animal life cycles. Photo labels and a picture glossary reinforce new vocabulary. The activity page reinforces comprehension and critical thinking. Use the ideas below to help children get even more out of their reading experience.

Before Reading

- Show the cover of the book to students. Ask: *What do you think this book is about?*
- Ask students to describe spines. Write their answers on the board.
- Look at the picture glossary. Discuss the meanings of the words.

During Reading

- Walk through the photos in the book. Discuss the different kinds of spines they see in the photos.
- Read the book aloud to students or have them read independently.
- After each spread, ask students to write the animal's name and what its spines do.

After Reading

- Ask the class to look at the glossary terms. Have students compare their guesses to the definitions.
- Use the What Do You Remember? activity on page 22 to help review the text.
- Discuss how spines help animals survive in nature.

Index

caterpillar 16
marine iguana 15
poison 16
porcupine 9
puffer fish 7
quills 9

scales 15
sea urchin 4
shell 4
short-horned lizard 12
spider 19
spiny anteater 11

Web Sites

San Diego Zoo's Animal Bytes: Echidna
http://www.sandiegozoo.org/animalbytes/t-echidna.html

Environmental Education for Kids. The Porcupine.
http://dnr.wi.gov/org/caer/ce/eek/critter/mammal/porcupine.htm

National Geographic Kids. Pufferfish.
http://kids.nationalgeographic.com/Animals/CreatureFeature/Pufferfish

Photo Credits
David Fleetham / Alamy, cover, 6, 22; Flip Nicklin/Minden Pictures/National Geographic Stock, 4–5, 22; George H.H. Huey/Alamy, 12–13, 22; IRA BLOCK/National Geographic Stock, 14, 21, 22; Kathie Atkinson/Photolibrary, 10, 22; Piotr Naskrecki/Minden Pictures/National Geographic Stock, 1, 18, 21; SMuller Smuller/Photolibrary, 8, 20, 22; THOMAS MARENT/MINDEN PICTURES/National Geographic Stock, 16–17, 20; Yali Shi/iStockphoto, 20